N/A Literary Magazine
Volume 1, Issue 2
Summer 2012

ISBN: 978-1-105-78130-8

Submitting to N/A:
We currently accept prose, poetry, and creative nonfiction submissions. Admissions are accepted anytime. Submit to NALiteraryMagazine@gmail.com

You can find more information about us at NALiteraryMagazine.tumblr.com, or by searching for us on Facebook as N/A Literary Magazine.

NO ASSHOLES!

Spring 2012 | Volume I | Issue 2

Prose

Poetry

King of the Hill
by Jordan Nisbet

Mnemonic
by Elizabeth Kerper

We Wade Through Waves and Moonlight
by Emily Roche

Twenty-Won
by Jessica Vorobel

New Jersey
by Cassandra Gillig

Sketch I
by Richard J. Rodriguez

Your Hairs on a Friday Morning
by M. Quinn Stifler

Neruda On A Saturday Morning
by C. Rhett Henry

This issue of N/A is dedicated to the memory of
Sean Patrick Murphy.

Letter From the Editors

Woah! Things look a little different around here, don't they? Don't fret; a little change now and then is a good thing.

The first thing you may have noticed is the name change: we are now (officially) N/A Literary Magazine. Some folks had sensitive eyeballs and didn't like the word "assholes" on their shelves. To this we shrug our shoulders and say the initials will do. We will always be No Assholes at heart. This is also the first time N/A has been published outside of our editors' bedrooms. While our inkjet printers are a bit mad that the only jobs they have now are essays for school, we think the rest of our reading audience will appreciate a well-made book.

Since our last issue, things have progressed rather quickly. Though our group is based out of Chicago, we are now receiving submissions from writers from all over the United States. Many of them are fresh-faced, and poised to take on the literary world. Exposing these writers to a wider reading audience is what this magazine is all about. If you like something you read in these pages, purchase a second copy to give to someone else. If you don't, purchase a second copy and reconsider your views. Either way, know that you are helping young writers of all different stripes and backgrounds practice their craft.

Happy writing,
The Editors

Flashlight

by Clare Stuber

When I was six
my mom told me
stargazing was no good.

So I dug in the
dirt instead
determined to
sing in the other direction.

But the dirt sung back.
And I laughed at the moon
and told her she was confusing

When I was young I wished
I was old.
I dreamt of wrinkly skin in
my back pocket and broken
baby teeth in my shoe.

I had a crush on god
thinking it would help.

Sleepwalking to the sky
my feet bled and my skin
melted into the dip of my hand.

And I laughed at the moon.
And my mom.

My grip tightened around my middle
and god yelled back.

King of the Hill

by Jordan Nisbet

When they fenced off
the concrete jungle
we called our playground
I resorted to using
your ribcage as monkey bars,
going from end to end
and always thinking you
were following right
behind me.

But you never
played back. You stood
in your quicksand box
and let me have my fun
without any question
and would always be smiling.
I'm sorry I helped you sink.

The fleeting glances
I would catch only
made me want to try
harder to be the King
of the Hill so I practiced
running up metal slides
for hours on end
I can't say whether
I did this for me,
or for you.

On the see-saw, as long
as our eyes were locked,
I could play by myself
for hours with the firm
belief that we were sitting
on the same pieces of wood
and metal and rust.

I still believe that I was right,
sometimes.

Mnemonic

by Elizabeth Kerper

Freshman year of high school, in the back
of a dingy classroom, I learned all
the places of the countries of Africa.

Strange words coated my mouth with chalk dust—
Rwanda, Uganda, Zimbabwe,
Senegal, Zaire— whispered over and

over, until the map became a
puzzle I could build with closed eyes. But
the way the landmasses slot together

slid from my mind, like water off pebbles,
along with the face of my first best
friend, though not the moist cloud of her breath in

my ear as she pressed newborn secrets
into my hands, jagged as palmfulls
of playground woodchips, and said not to tell.

I haven't forgotten the weight of
not telling—lead in my pockets—but
the secrets are gone, like Africa, like

the demons that once lurked in my dark
room. The litany of their hiding
spots still scrolls across my mind— how shadows

flared against my curtains and closet—
and how my taut, terrified fingers
carved vicious half-moons deep into the sides

of my mattress, but the monsters are
faceless, lost. It's strange, to know you have
forgotten, to remember forgetting,

but stranger still is wondering what
you do not remember losing, if beyond
your shadows float echoes, patient as ghosts.

Parts

by Eric Boyd

1.

Naked, dripping wet, I stood in front of the guard.

"Last name, Anderson; first name, Fredrick?"

"Yes," I said, meekly.

"Squat down, like taking a shit."

I bent down, almost slipping on the floor. I caught myself and squatted.

"Cough."

I coughed.

The guard looked at me. "Come on and COUGH."

I did. It was louder.

"Now stand up, turn around, spread your ass."

I did.

"Okay, turn back around, look at me. Open up your mouth with your hands, show me under your tongue, behind your teeth."

I did.

"Great. Thanks. Welcome to jail, how did your ass taste?"

2.

Luther told me to kill a mouse stuck in a glue trap. Him and I worked together at the jail. He took care of supplies for the jail and I handled the trash. He hated mice. I did not.

"Did you— Woah!" he yelled. "What're you doing, Fredrick?"

"I'm loosening the trap with soap."

"Why?"

"So he'll get free," I said, looking at the mouse.

"Those things have the fucking plague!"

"We're the plague," I said.

"What?"

"We're the mice."

"Anderson, you're as crazy as everyone says!" Luther shouted.

"That's fine."

"Even if you let it go, it'll die after a day."

"How's that?"

"Mice in traps get frightened to death. Their widdle hearts can't take it," he mocked.

"That's fine, too."

Luther walked out, shaking his head.

I had no idea what I would do when I left this place.

3.

Me and another inmate were scraping metal at the old county morgue.

Conan, the guard escorting us, was a bulky, New Jersey-type.

He was always joking. He picked up two rusty, blood caked knives from an examining table, the knives they cut people with, looking like small machetes. He put them behind him, like an 'X'. Conan was always trying to be funny. He pulled the knives from behind his back. "Hey! I'm like a ninja with these— Aw fuck!"

A knife had sliced into his knuckles. He ran off to clean the cut.

He was so funny. The other inmate and I laughed. Ha.

4.

Aside from the school in Iowa, where I wrote little journal pieces, I had no experience with formal writing. I did screenplays, but never prose or poetry. I screwed around, but I didn't feel anything I wrote was worthwhile.

During my first class in the jail however, I learned that writing wasn't very hard, or that I was at least better at it than most inmates at a county penitentiary.

"You're a natural," the jail writing teacher said.

"Natural what?"

"Don't be silly; you were born a writer!"

"Oh boy."

"Sometimes fate tests us, Fredrick."

"I guess."

5.

We drove through the city, going home, from the jail.

The drive was strange. Outside, it had started raining, neon dripping down the windshield, exploding with the wipers. The wind was blowing, rocking the car as we went. The rocking made me sleepy.

Eyes half-closed, every streetlamp was very bright, yellow. Colors were brighter, deeper than I was used to. It all melted with the rain against the windshield. Every car, motorcycle, bike was very fast. Anybody walking on the sidewalks blurred by. Everything blurred. Looking out at the city, it looked so different.

"It's okay," I said to myself.

6.

The first few days back at home were good.

My father, Daniel, and I were getting along okay. He was getting fatter, never leaving the living room couch, sleeping on the couch and eating in front of the TV, watching old Super bowls he had taped, sometimes porno hidden under the couch cushions. We had nothing in common except music; he liked eighties hair metal and oldies, and I tolerated hearing it while in the same room as him.

After a month Daniel tried murdering my mother; I gave him a black eye and he kicked me out of the house.

We Wade Through Waves and Moonlight

by Emily Roche

And tonight is an evening of placid contagion –
with power in the fiber of the bones of my hands.
And tonight, if I could, I'd sail for the horizon
with you at my side, on my seas, in my lands.
And I think that we'd go 'till our sails caught the gust of
some monstrous wind that sought never to fade.
And, blown off of our course, we'd set flame to the map
because really, it's better, in fact, that we'd strayed.
And soon we would land at the end of the world,
as our hands kept the sun from our wanderers' eyes-
and we'd climb from the decks onto uncharted land
and roll over these shores where the tide never dries.
And we'd shout to the light that fell down from the skies.
And we'd take to the summits
where the spark never dies.
But tonight, I've no sails fit for an adventure-
and tonight there's no wind to serenade with its groans.
So tonight I'll stay in, and I'll stare to the moon
with my grin on my face, and your grin in my bones.

Twenty-Won

by Jessica Vorobel

I find myself at twenty-one
Acutely aware of the sips I take.
Your father was an alcoholic, you know.
You need to be careful about these things.
What mother fails to mention is
He was a recovering alcoholic, to me, always.
A sponsor to those struggling.
A beacon of light for those in the blackest darkness.

Today I found myself
in a staring contest
with a half drunk
bottle of wine at two
in the afternoon,
all the while picturing
my father's dead
and decaying body.

We hit a stalemate,
the bottle and I.
A few sips here and there,
but in the end,
the bottle went unfinished.

In fact, I'm staring right now
at a half drunk glass of
South African white wine
from this afternoon.

So who won? Who is winning?
Earlier this evening
I went to the pubs
with a few friends
and had a few pints.
Who is winning? Who won?

New Jersey

by Cassandra Gillig

Searching for you
in such large hell, I am
Robert Lowell with breasts
and a heart.

I want to mourn the
color of this river; it will
be where we first find that
small, white crosses are

buoyant in reflected
verdigris. Expansive, we
occupy January. Someone
(maybe me) will use it

against us. Swaddled by
hotel room sheets, there is no
optimal word that functions
to describe my container.

You are longing in this
sterile segregation. The tide
is blank and you are yielding.
I flood all dirt waters.

Dislocated second place,
my hands like borders. We
carry nothing through the
interim; in Camden, I elapse.

Sketch I

by Richard J. Rodriguez

Where are her ears supposed to be?
                    I don't know.
                    I've never seen her.

Her belly kind of goes out like this.
I don't know how to make a crotch.
                    What is her arm doing?
                    What is she doing?

Now she's a   hermaphrodite.
                    Dissected eyes—
                    penetrating.

Who should you be?
                    The Milky Pirate?

Mmm. What does your nose look like?
                    Pyramidal. Pyramicidal.
                    Like Alexander the Great.

Now you have brawny shoulders
and excessive nipples.
                    Thank you.

You resemble chimeras—
hawk-man, beetle-man, ram-man; they're not what I had in mind.

               Lots n' lots of jets n' planes —
               n' serpents.

I can never figure out where the ears are supposed to go
and my shoulder alignment is off.
                    It's Jabba the Hutt
                    with Eraserhead hair.

Now you're cupping his breasts. He likes it, see?
                    He needs a smile.
                    And more teeth.

You run your claw through his luminous beard,
his hairy shoulders.
                                    His seven rows of teeth!

I really fucked up your face. I'm sorry.
                                    I, he   is ravishing.

He's got this   what is this called?
                                    An Egyptian rat tail?

No, it's something else.
                                    It's a canary   with a penis.

He is clenching his breasts in the mirror
                              and he is   stunning.

for AW

Your Hairs on a Friday Morning

by M. Quinn Stifler

Here we are early in the morning and your hairs
are telling me jokes, awkwardly interjecting
expletives into casual conversation. They think
they're a teenager sitting at the kids table, a cadaver
reading the daily news on the four train.

We've been painted in bed, distant eyes,
indifferent hands, thinking of dead family:
the people who we won't miss until guilted
into remorse, The Christmas lights above us
that remind us of every song that mentions
Christmas lights. I knead your damp clay curls,
laughing at how intimidated I am by their texture,
by the god forsakenly ugly frame which surrounds us.

In your bedroom, I am laughing at your hairs turning
grey as a Saturday at Pike Street, speaking in French
when they know I don't comprehend, making toast
at midnight. I swear I met your hairs at the market
yesterday. They slipped me a dollar while I waited
at the check-out, to let them go ahead in line.

Neruda on a Saturday Morning
by C. Rhett Henry

Ah,
you've
been in
my kiss cemetery
for what seems
like...
Forever!

Pills

by Haley Green

We wanted to sit outside, but it had started raining, and mom's knee was acting up. We sat in the kitchen then and set up the chessboard in there. It hadn't changed much since I was little, with the crazily checkered floor, the olive green stove, and laminate topped table.

"I haven't played in so long," mom said. She was looking so ashy and crinkled, and her hair, once blonde, now nearly white. She smiled at me, exposing only a sliver of teeth, a habit born out of her embarrassment of the gap between her two front incisors. I'd inherited the same Chiclet front teeth, but not the shame.

"Neither have I," I said. I sorted the white pieces from the black. I always played black, since mom first taught me when I was six, but I decided I'd play white this time.

Mom glanced up at me from lining up her pieces on the board. "You know, I don't think you've been here since I converted your old bedroom into a studio. It must have been two months."

"I'm here now."

"Of course. And I'm glad to have you. I'd be even gladder if it were under different circumstances, but all the same."

"Mom," I said, setting down the rook I was about to place into position in the second row.

"What?" she said, showing me that small smile. It made her look so apologetic and girlish. "Oh, come on, don't look at me like that. This is life, this is being an adult. Things don't always work out."

"Yeah, I think I got that when I was fired." I smiled at mom with all my teeth.

Mom raised her eyebrows at me.

"I was kidding. I know, I – Let's just play."

"I didn't think you were that upset over it."

"What do you mean?"

"Well, you just haven't talked about it very much. It seems like you're just going about business as usual, but I know that can't really be the case."

"It's fine. I don't really want to be stuck copywriting for the rest of my life. And I'm doing fine *not* thinking about it."

"Why not be a copywriter?"

"Because. I need a change of pace. It's not important." I had never been certain if dad cared about my interest in writing, but I knew he'd always begrudged my career as a copywriter. Something about wasted potential or life wasted. It had kept me awake at nights sometimes, especially around when I was fired, wondering if he was right.

"Don't you think it's bad for you to hold things in like that?"

I could feel the metallic crackle and hum under my skin, the warmth creeping up, the itchy, wet, warmth. It was pushing outward and upward, and so had to swallow. I pushed a pawn forward one square. "No. It's better this way."

Mom pushed forward her pawn. "That's what *I* used to think. I try not to talk to you kids too much about your dad, but it wasn't easy for me, you know. I just held it in."

"Sometimes that's what you have to do," I said.

"No – no, I learned my lesson. After your father died – I know it's crude to say this – but after he died, I felt free for the first time since I don't remember when."

It wasn't that I didn't know what mom was talking about. I remembered the way he would every now and then realize the people he was surrounded by – not scholars like himself, who were brilliant, prodigies, geniuses, explorers, philosophers, and artists. We were his wife and daughters. Children. Distraction. There wasn't a time when I remember him not being disappointed. But mom didn't look at it the way I did, and so it was always easier to be dismissive. "Yeah, well, dad was an asshole."

"Hm. I wouldn't say that. He just liked things a certain way."

I pushed forward my rook.

Mom tutted and said, "I know you two didn't see eye to eye. You were always more like me."

"It's your move, Mom."

Mom looked at me like she was trying to swallow a laugh. She moved her bishop, and put my pawn on the table beside the board. I noticed then that her red nail polish was looking chipped. Mom took care of her nails. She went into the salon every other week to get them done, with the acrylic, and the white tips, and the pink or the red varnish. Her hands otherwise were muscular, not little and slender, and I suppose that's why she'd always gotten them done like that. Even with all that work, to make her hands look feminine, she'd spent hours in the garden, pulling weeds, pouring mulch, trimming the rosemary and hedges. Dad wasn't around to do these things, especially in his later years, when he got dementia, so mom did it all.

"Have you been gardening?" I said.

Mom held her hand out, and frowned at the crooked ridges of the nail polish. "It's the damn wind. It's been blowing all these seeds around. You wouldn't be*lieve* what the yard looked like last weekend." She laid her palm flat on the table, and looked up at me. "Is there a reason why you don't want to talk about getting fired?" It was so curious the way she could look at me. I could be such a small, interesting creature, the way I swallowed my fury every morning, like a pill. Fury wasn't a pill, it was an ointment that you rubbed into your dry knuckles. Mom looked at me with her slivered mouth, wondering, "Don't you know that? Have I taught you nothing?"

"It's over. I have nothing else to say about it." I moved my knight forward, and claimed one of her pawns.

"Ah, I see," said mom. She was sitting there, nearly luxuriating in my discomfort, with her shoulders rolled back, eyes hooded. It somehow reminded me of that afternoon two weeks before dad died, after the dementia had nearly swallowed him whole, rendering him stupid and blurry eyed. His face looked smudged in those last two weeks. Mom had never looked better.

"What?" I said. I was starting to feel my hair stick to the back of my neck, and my face was hot.

"I just want you to know I'm there for you. I'm worried about you."

Dad had been sitting at the table eating a sandwich mom had made for him. He ate a few slow bites, and then took off the top piece of bread to wipe off the mustard and mayo on the edge of the plate, even though he'd always liked mustard and mayo before. He continued to pull off the crusts, until his sandwich was just a white little square. Silhouetted as he was at the table, he looked smaller than I'd ever seen him, shoulders rounded, elbows tucked in, chin soft. Mom was standing at the counter near him. I was in the doorway, half hidden in the dark of the hallway. I could almost hear the click of her nails on the counter.

“Just be honest. Don’t hold it in, is all I’m saying,” said mom, her silver eyes narrowing.

I don’t remember now why that afternoon, I’d stopped there in the doorway. Mom had been just standing there, in a red cocktail dress, with her arms crossed under her breasts, watching dad eat.

“I’m fine,” I said. My voice sounded like it was coming from somewhere far away -- somewhere miles underwater. It was only a silver bubble rising from the dark.

Dad had looked up at mom with his cowlick of thinning grey hair and blank baby eyes. I thought weirdly that the look on her face when she met his gaze was affectionate, with her eyes so sensuously halved by eyelids. She moved away from the counter, closer to dad, hands at her sides, hips squared, and I think she almost smiled -- just the razor edge of it gleamed for a moment in the light streaming in from the window. She extended a hand midair, as if she were sticking it out a window, to test the weather. The smile dropped from her face, and her lips thinned. Her open hand swung down, hard across dad’s face.

Dad was quiet, his mouth slackened. He peered up at her, with eyes so docile and flat I don’t even think he knew what had happened.

“It’s not good for you. You’ll snap one day, I guarantee it,” mom said.

I sucked in a deep breath through the mouth.

Mom claimed my knight.

Poem for Billy Tipton

by Christopher Rife

The same fingers that floated
across ivory keys in clubs, and stroked
the hair of women who chose ignorance,
and built fires on family camping trips

also wrapped thick strands of canvas
around unwanted breasts
to bound down evidence
that the story you told was less than true.

When your children looked on as
paramedics uncovered what was hidden
from them for all those years,

I hope they remembered your melodies,
the strength of your palms,
the love that lined your hands.

While On The Subject

by Alex Jewell

I remember hugging the rails,
A note below water level,
As meaning took me down with heavy breath
And shallow sips reminded me of fulfilling gulps
Served from ornate cups:
A survivor, nonetheless,
Telling stories from the depths.

We're all thrill seekers until high tide;
Wise until proven otherwise;
Human caskets so full of life,
With the memories of goldfish;
No mystery until surprise.

Is it that much to swallow?
Ignoring beckoning inquiry
As it echoes throughout our hollow.
Empty, it drips,
Yet still more empty follows.

Edward Hopper's *Nighthawks* Interpreted by Children

by Samy Sabh

I take my morning over-easy on
top a heap of hashed meat. She takes
hers sunny-side up with a happy
faced banana pancake, sliding the
sliced banana pieces from
a smile
to a frown.

She says-	*This is how I've felt, Sam.*
I say-	Let's commence the patching process,
	Fix it up—talk it out—stitch the wound
She says-	and kid ourselves?
I say-	ourselves is just kids.

She says
You're so breakfast for dinner
so nevertheless
so unabashedly unabashed
She says
You're so dirty soap
so naughty tongue with a
salacious sting.

Oh, we're cookin' now.

I say
You're so numb feet
so natural disaster
so flash flood of endorphins

leaving Katrina lookin' like a
kiddy pool
I say
You're so heavy sedative
so rug burned knees with denim
caught around the ankles like a
hog-tied damsel moaning on the
train tracks; Save me!
I can't feel my feet
I can't feel my feet
but god damn is it ever time to run.
I say
Oh sweet spoonful! I've missed you
and your catastrophes
but I fear that I am no longer the
crafty bandit that saves you
in the nick of time
I am the barreling locomotive
with roaring momentum; treacherous
and unforgiving.

She says
Remember that time
we jumped from the plane

Pulled our parachutes a
thousand feet too late for
that extra moment of free fall?

I miss the danger
That narrow thread

I say
You're so mood ring
She says
You're so wrong about yourself
I say
Fuck You!
She says
Fuck me!
I say

look.

If there is one thing that I wish
I could assure you, it would be this-

I will work ceaselessly to ensure that when you die It will be on a mattress of thunderous orgasms
And silver dollars. I will carry you down a hallway
Lined with daisy-chains and remorse and I will sing

I'll give you today if you give me tomorrow

I'll give you twenty years if you give me twenty that follow.

And people will say

She was loved. She was loved good and hard.

And then they will cry, as they have never been loved

So good.
And so hard.

But I can't-

I can't promise you this because I am the locomotive with barreling momentum. She says

Then let's kid ourselves
As ourselves—just kids.

And then I agree.

CONTRIBUTORS NOTES

Eric Boyd was born on October 16th, at 3:33AM, 1988 in North Carolina. He briefly studied at the Maharishi University of Management in Fairfield, Iowa. Boyd is the literary editor of Pork & Mead magazine; he also helps edit the Newer York literary magazine. A winner of the PEN American 2012 Prison Writing contest, Boyd's work has also been featured in several journals, both online and in print, including the Rusty Nail, Fourth River, and Velvet Blory; his first collection of short stories, Whiskey Sour, was released in the spring of 2012 by Nervous Puppy Publishing. The collection will soon enter its second printing. Eric Boyd currently lives in Homestead, Pennsylvania.

This is **C. Rhett Henry**'s first publication! Hurrah! He is studying creative writing and philosophy at Emory University in Atlanta and has lived in the Metro area his whole life. His interests include (but are thankfully not limited to) soul and funk music, American conspiracy theorists, and the painter Giorgio de Chirico. He is currently working on his first novel, an *Odyssey* homage set in an alternate 1960s.

Haley Green does not like it when people misspell her name as "Hayley". She did not submit a biography. A pox upon her, but only a tiny one.

Cassandra Gillig is 19 and lives in Chicago. She has chapbooks forthcoming from NAP and Love Symbol Press. Ole, bitch, ole.

Jessica Vorobel was born and raised in Cleveland, used to live in London and studies geography in Chicago. She's not an asshole, but she is a bit geographically schizophrenic.

Jordan Nisbet is 19 years old. His home is Toronto, ON, Canada.

Clare Stuber attends DePaul University. She did not submit a biography. Maybe she doesn't like writing in third person.

Emily Roche is a native of Buffalo NY, and just finished her freshman year at NYU, where she is double-majoring in Russian and English. She has been writing poetry since she was ten; her favorite poets are T.S. Eliot and Allen Ginsberg. Her favorite authors include Fitzgerald, Dostoevsky, and Nabokov. Other than writing, her hobbies include swing dancing and playing the accordion.

M. Quinn Stifler studies English and Women's/Gender Studies with a minor in LGBTQ Studies at DePaul University. Stifler has published poetry and short fiction in a number of local Michigan journals as well as their own zines. On the weekends, they work as an editor and title-ghost-writer for In Our Words: A Salon for Queers and Co. They're interested in radical politics, queer everythings, folk punk, word play, and aesthetically pleasing living spaces. E-mail them anything ever at mqstifler@me.com.

Christopher Rife is a junior at DePaul University, studying Communication and Media and Creative Writing. He is Editor-In-Chief of N/A Literary Magazine (Editor's Note: this very publication!), and a contributor to The Polkadodge Organization. His short plays have been published by SpeechGeek and Mushroomcloud Press, and his poetry is forthcoming in *Threshold.* He is current a Programming Assistant at 826CHI, where he teaches kids about poetry without putting them to sleep. Outside of comedy and writing, his interests include unsolicited karaoke, wearing fake mustaches over his real one, and capybaras. He can be contacted at CNRife@gmail.com

Samy Sabh is sometimes withdrawn as a modest observer and other times he is mouthy and rather abrasive. He is a lover of many things and despiser of many things. He is a dedicated musician, a dedicated poet, and a mildly sedated undergrad that eats cold pizza for breakfast and has an endless fear of the future. His work is of sweeping landscapes, Golden Retrievers, and sex. Samy wants to thank N/A for taking interest in his craft, and also wants to thank Chicago, his friends, his lover, and his family for all of the ceaseless inspiration.

Alex Jewell did not submit a biography. Perhaps he has secrets to hide. He attends DePaul University.

Elizabeth Kerper lives in Chicago and studies English at DePaul University. She looks forward to getting her life together someday, but in the meantime, she can generally be found sitting quietly in the corner with her nose stuck in a book. Writing poetry and fiction is her favorite form of procrastination. She can be contacted at elizkerper@gmail.com.

Acknowledgments

We would like to thank our parents, for without their chromosomes, none of this would be possible. Also, their support makes things easier too.

The Editors would also like to thank the Creative Writing department at DePaul University. The professors and writers of that department are largely responsible for much of the content of this magazine. Props.

Thanks should also be given to the staff of 826CHI, for their continued encouragement and self-publishing knowledge. They do great things for Chicago's youth, so you should support them as well. Find them at 826CHI.org.

The photos that grace our cover were taken by the wonderful Anna Hollow. Her work will soon be taking the world by storm. More of her work can be seen on her Flickr page, or at AnnaHollow.tumblr.com.

A final thanks should go to the readers and writers who are spending their valuable time purchasing, reading, and being amazed by the work within. You guys are pretty cool.

www.ingramcontent.com/pod-product-compliance
Ingram Content Group UK Ltd.
Pitfield, Milton Keynes, MK11 3LW, UK
UKHW051133260726
13967UKWH00010B/3026